The Perfect Pet

For Adam

First published in Great Britain in 1999 by Andersen Press Ltd.,
20 Vauxhall Bridge Road, London SW1V 2SA. This paperback edition first published in 2000
by Andersen Press Ltd. Published in Australia by Random House Australia Pty.,
20 Alfred Street, Milsons Point, Sydney, NSW 2061.All rights reserved.
Colour separated in Italy by Fotoriproduzioni Grafiche, Verona.
Printed and bound in Italy by Grafiche AZ, Verona.

10   9   8   7   6   5   4   3   2   1

British Library Cataloguing in Publication Data available.

ISBN 0 86264 102 0

This book has been printed on acid-free paper

The Perfect Pet

Peta Coplans

Andersen Press
London

A hen went into a pet shop.
"May I help you?" asked the pig behind the counter.

"I want a pet," said the hen.
"That's why I'm here."

"How about a mouse?" said the pig.
"Very small, quiet, a perfect pet."
"No, no, no," said the hen,
"a mouse is too squeaky."

"How about a rabbit?" said the pig.
"Rabbits never squeak and they're cuddly pets."
    "No, no, no," said the hen, "a rabbit isn't right . . .
What's that, over there?"

"That," said the pig, "is a fox."
"I'll take him," said the hen.
"He's just what I want."

"She's crazy," muttered the pig.
"Dotty as a doughnut . . .
Do you want him wrapped, Madam?"

"No, thank you," said the hen.
"We're walking home."
　　She paid the pig, took the fox by the paw,
and off they went.

They had only gone a little way, when the fox sat down.

"I'm thirsty," he said. "Foxes need plenty of lemonade to drink."

"I didn't know that," said the hen. "I'll make you some lemonade when we get home."

"I have to rest," said the fox a little later.
"Foxes can't walk very far."
"I didn't know that," said the hen . . .

"Sit in my shopping trolley.
I'll push you."

The hen was hot and tired by the time
they reached her house.

She made a jug of lemonade,
but the fox drank it all before she
could pour herself a glassful.

"I'm hungry," said the fox. "Where's the pie?"
"Pie?" said the hen. "Is that what foxes eat?
I didn't know that!"
"Foxes love pie," said the fox.
"Can you make pastry?"

"Of course, right away," said the hen.
"Hurry it up," said the fox. "I'm starving."

"Hens love pie, too," said the hen. "Apple,
blackberry . . . worm pie is my favourite.
What sort of pie do you like?" she asked the fox.

"You'll see," said the fox, as he popped the pastry into a pie dish and tossed in a few sliced mushrooms. "It's a surprise."

"This IS interesting," said the hen. "What's next?"

"Next," said the fox, "is a nice, fat hen –
not too clever."

"That's me!" said the hen. "I'm nice and fat
and not too clever."

"Well," said the fox, "what are you waiting for? Jump in!"

"Good grief!" squawked the hen.
"You were making CHICKEN pie!
I didn't know THAT!"

And she whacked the fox on the head
with a saucepan, threw him in her shopping trolley,
and marched right back to the pet shop.

"You were right," said the hen to the pig
behind the counter. "I don't want a fox."

"Well, well," said the pig. "Do you see anything else you like?"

"I like that one over there," said the hen.
"That's exactly the pet I want. Wrap it up, please."
"Anything you say!" said the pig . . .

as he wrapped up the crocodile.

More Andersen Press paperback picture books!